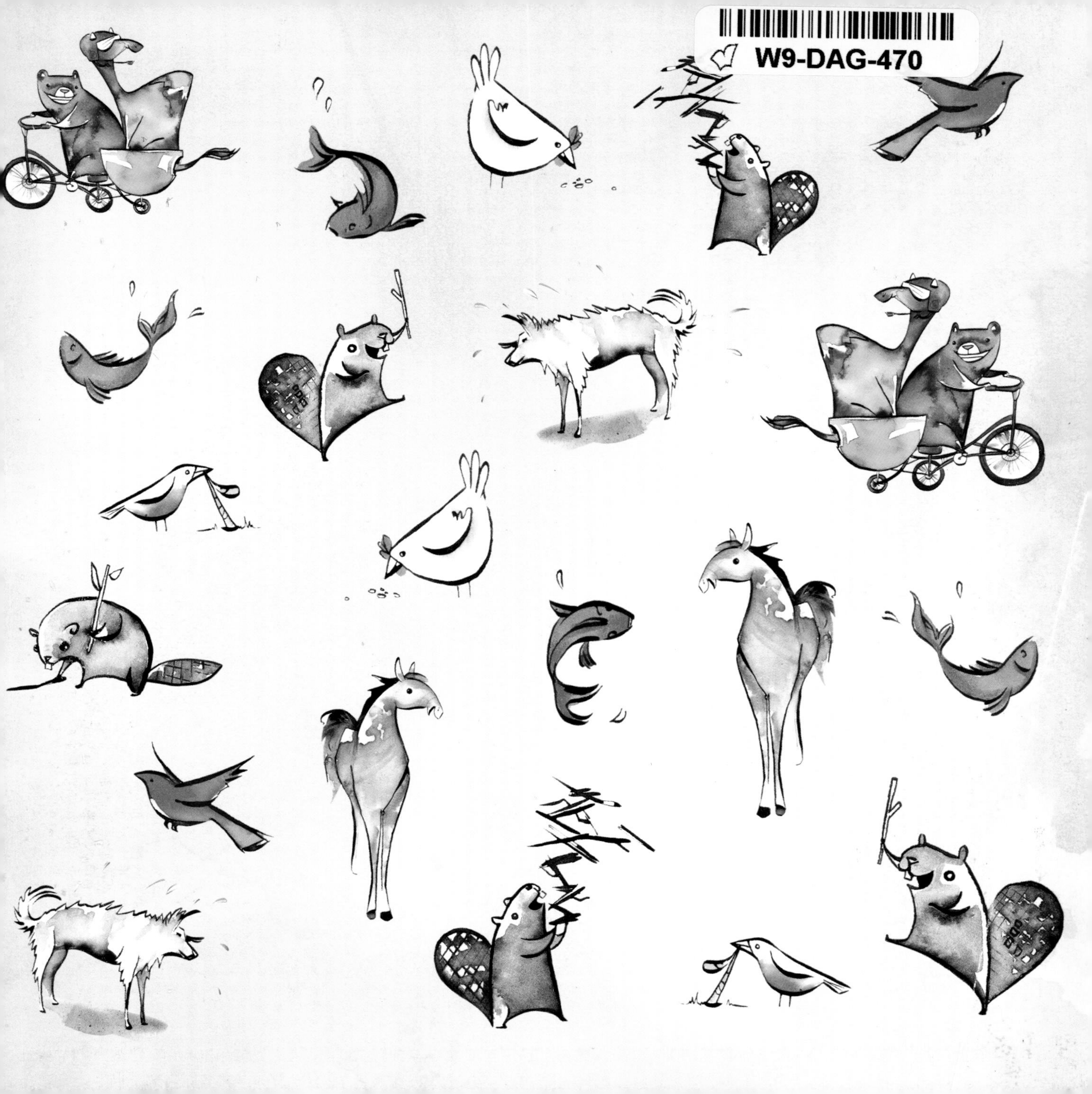

With love to my parents, whose wit and wisdom
have kept me on my toes and always reaching for the stars. —T.J.

For my family and all of their love and support. —Emma

First published in 2009 by Simply Read Books
www.simplyreadbooks.com

Library and Archives Canada Cataloguing in Publication

James, Tamara
The world is your oyster / written by Tamara James ; illustrated by Emma SanCartier.

ISBN 978-1-897476-22-2

1. Idioms--Juvenile fiction. I. SanCartier, Emma II. Title.

PS8619.A6614W67 2009 jC813'.6 C2009-901952-3

We gratefully acknowledge for their financial support of our publishing program the Canada Council for the Arts, the BC Arts Council, and the Government of Canada through the Book Publishing Industry Development Program (BPIDP).

Book design by Sara Gillingham.

10 9 8 7 6 5 4 3 2 1

Printed in Singapore.

THE WORLD IS YOUR OYSTER

By Tamara James
Illustrated by Emma SanCartier

Some days your world is

raining cats and dogs.

you feel like you're

up

to

your

neck

in

alligators,

and you're moving

at a snail's pace.

Other days you feel

like a fish out of water

or a 

bull in a china shop.

Someone's

got

your goat,

the cat's
got your tongue,

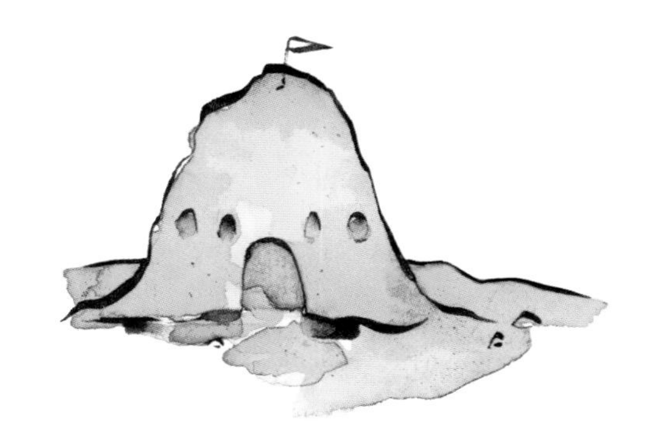

and all you want to do is
bury your head
in the sand.

Before you

make

a

mountain

out

of

a

molehill,

chicken out,

or throw yourself
to the lions,

remember what
a little bird
once told me . . .

You need to

grab the tiger

by the tail.

Take the bull
by the horns.

Be an eager beaver

and the

early bird that

gets the worm.

Because, in the end,

it's as plain as the hump

on a camel's back:

If you grin and bear it,

always go
the
whole hog,

and reach for the stars,

the world
is your oyster!

And that is
straight from the
horse's mouth!